This igloo book belongs to:

....

igloobooks

Published in 2020
by Igloo Books Ltd
Cottage Farm
Sywell
NN6 0BJ
www.igloobooks.com

0620 002
2 4 6 8 10 9 7 5 3
ISBN 978-1-83903-301-8

Original story by Kenneth Grahame
Retold by Stephanie Moss
Illustrated by Sumi Collina

Designed by Justine Ablett
Edited by Stephanie Moss

Printed and manufactured in China

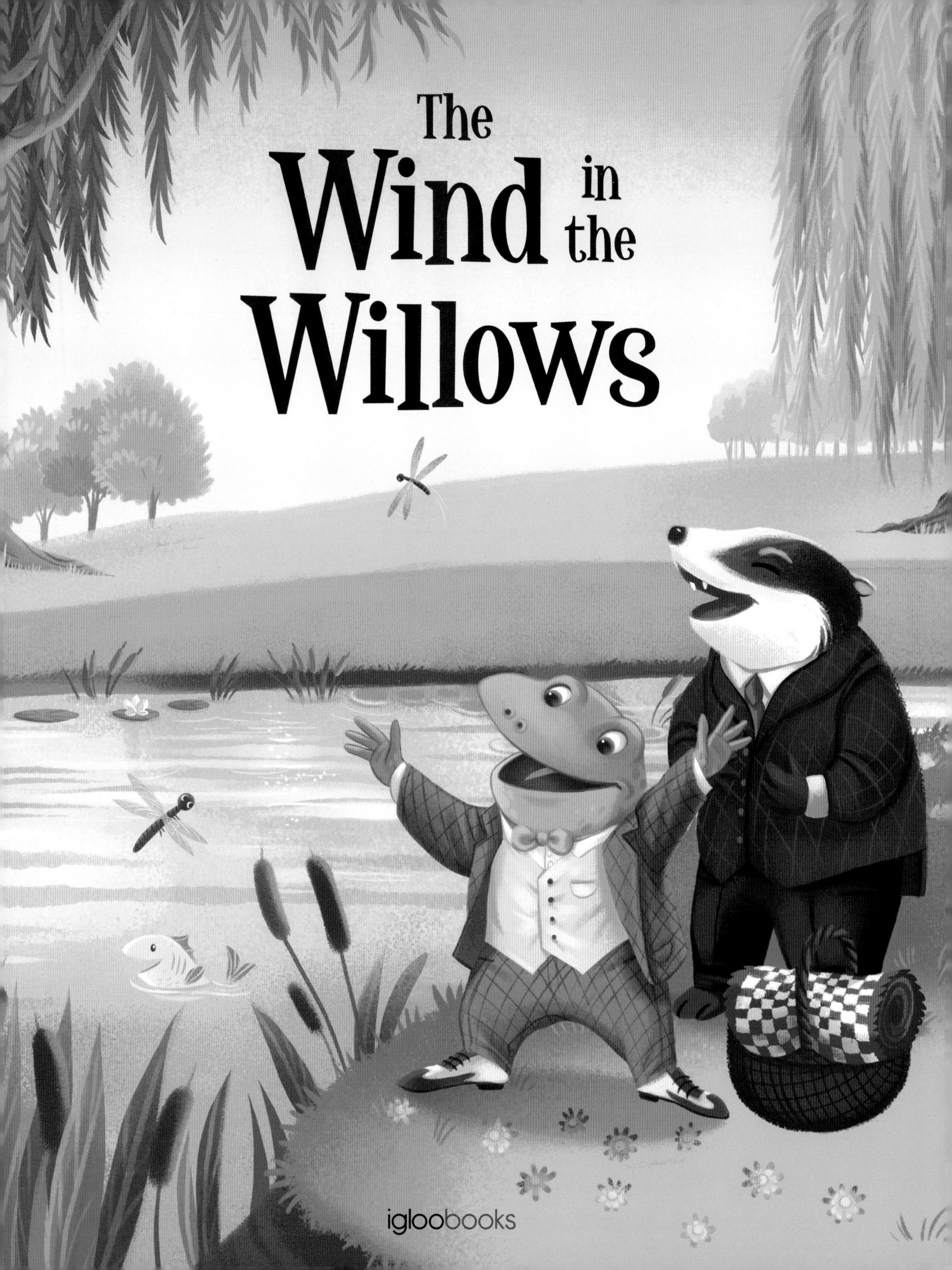
The Wind in the Willows
igloobooks

Mole lived in a gloomy underground house all by himself. One morning, he was tired of spring-cleaning, so he headed out into the sunlight. At the riverbank, he met Ratty. **"Do you want to come for a boat ride?"** he called. Mole had never been in a boat before, so he stepped in, eagerly.

Later that day, they had a picnic with Badger and Otter, who told Mole stories about their friend Mr Toad. When it was time to go home, Ratty asked Mole, **"Would you like to come and stay with me?"** Mole was so pleased, he could hardly speak.

Ratty spent the summer teaching Mole to row and swim, but one day, Mole asked to meet Mr Toad. **"I've heard so much about him,"** he said. So, they rowed down the river until the magnificent Toad Hall appeared.

Toad showed them his brand-new yellow caravan. **"We must take it out this afternoon!"** he cried.

"I'm not going anywhere," said Ratty, who hated leaving the river, but Toad soon convinced them to go on an adventure on the open road.

"How splendid to see you!" cried Toad, welcoming them with open arms.

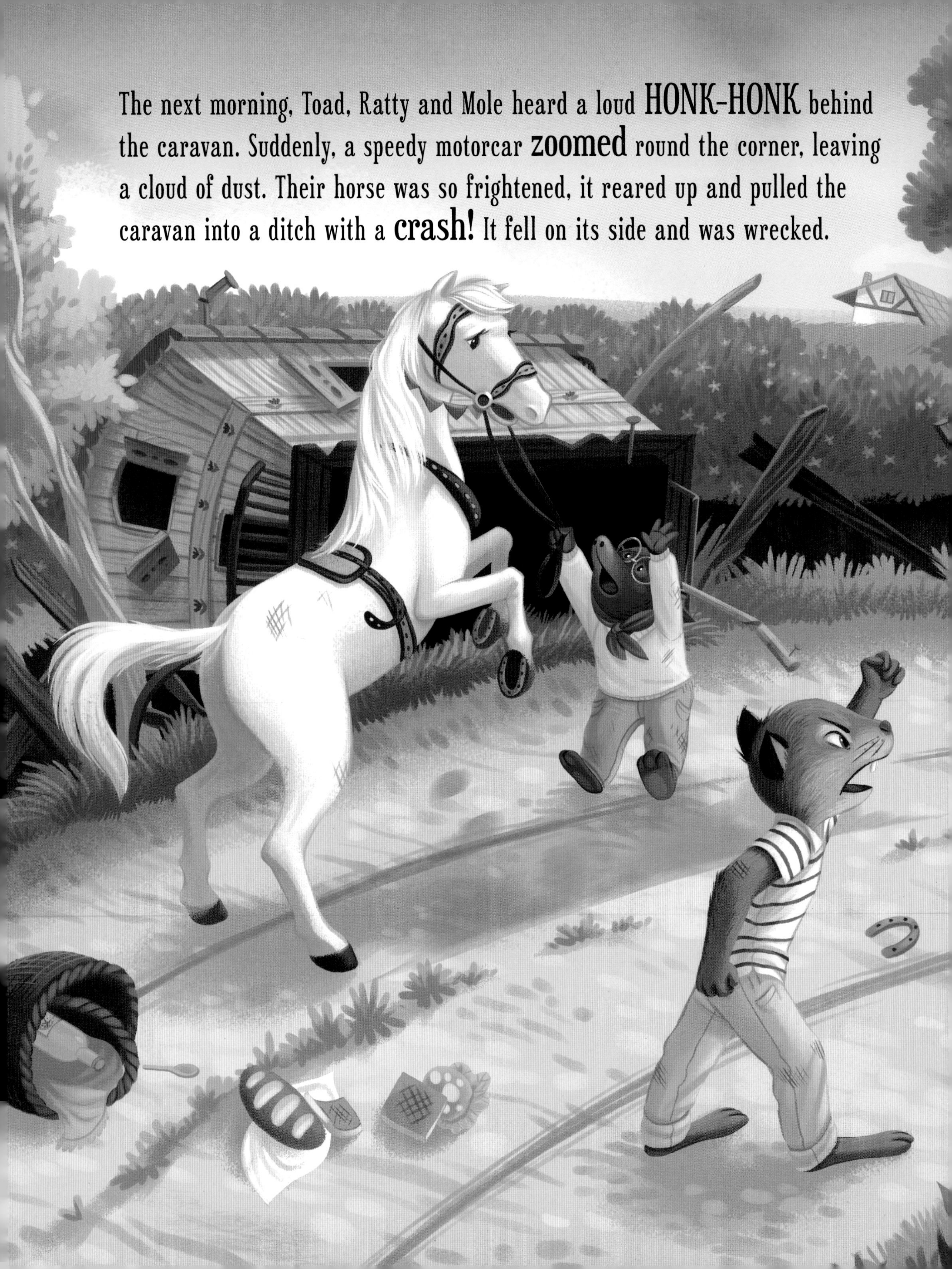

The next morning, Toad, Ratty and Mole heard a loud HONK-HONK behind the caravan. Suddenly, a speedy motorcar zoomed round the corner, leaving a cloud of dust. Their horse was so frightened, it reared up and pulled the caravan into a ditch with a crash! It fell on its side and was wrecked.

"You villains!" cried angry Ratty at the drivers, but Toad couldn't take his eyes off the disappearing vehicle. **"Are you coming to fix the caravan, Toad?"** asked Ratty.

"Oh no, I'm done with that forever!" he replied. The next thing they heard, Toad had bought his very own expensive motorcar.

As the months passed, the weather grew cold and Ratty spent most of his time sleeping. So, Mole went to visit Badger, but got lost in the Wild Wood. Ratty searched for hours until he finally found his friend. Every path looked exactly the same in the snow, and there seemed to be no way out.

Suddenly, to Mole's surprise, Ratty cried,
"Look, a doormat. Hooray!"
Finally, after digging in the snow, they
found an iron bell by a dark green door.
There was a shiny, gold sign next to it.

"Come in," said Badger,
when he answered the door.
"You must be freezing."

Kind Badger helped Ratty and Mole get warm and gave them a delicious supper. Then, he asked about Toad. **"He's had seven car crashes,"** said Ratty, shaking his head. **"I'm sure he'll hurt himself again or get into more trouble."** They decided to visit Toad the next day.

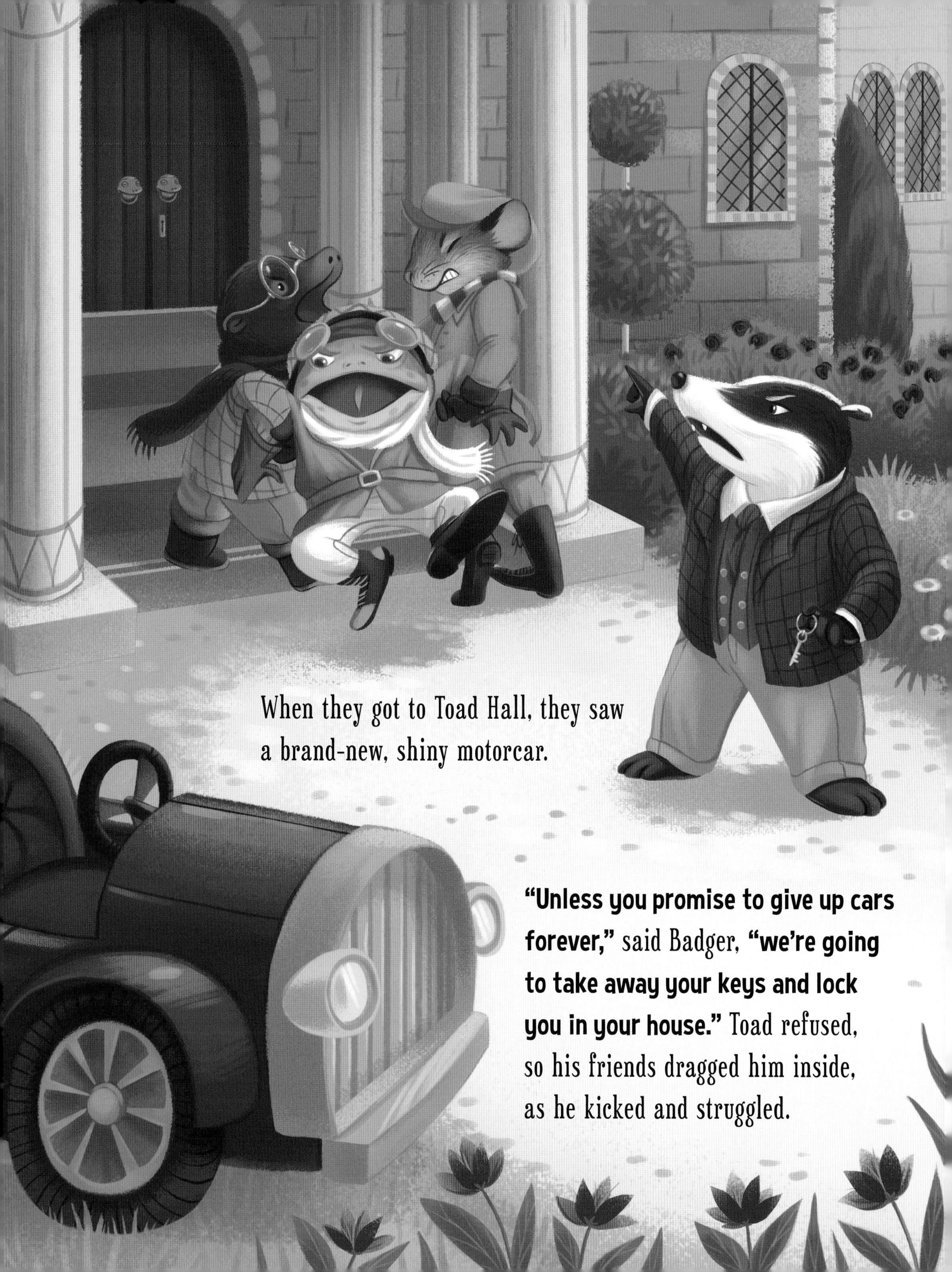

When they got to Toad Hall, they saw a brand-new, shiny motorcar.

"Unless you promise to give up cars forever," said Badger, **"we're going to take away your keys and lock you in your house."** Toad refused, so his friends dragged him inside, as he kicked and struggled.

Each animal took turns to guard Toad until, one morning, he asked Ratty to fetch the doctor. **"He must be really ill,"** thought Ratty. He locked the door and ran to the village, while sneaky Toad **hopped** out of bed, made his sheets into a rope and climbed out of the window!

Toad marched into town. He felt very proud of himself for escaping. Suddenly, he heard a **BEEP-BEEP**, as a car stopped nearby. No sooner had the owner got out than Toad found himself at the wheel, **roaring** and **racing** down the country lanes faster than ever before.

"Woo-hoo!" he cried.

It wasn't long before Toad was caught and sent to prison for stealing the car. **"Twenty years for you,"** said the judge, as Toad was led to the dungeon.

"Cheer up, Toad," said the guard's kind daughter, who loved animals. **"I know how you can get out of here!"**

The girl helped Toad switch clothes with her aunt, who was the prison's washerwoman. Dressed in his clever disguise, Toad walked straight out of the prison gates.

"I'm free!" thought Toad, heading to the train station. He had no money for a ticket, but the kind driver gave him a ride.

Then, Toad heard shouting behind him. **"Stop, stop!"** cried a train full of policemen.

"Please save me," begged Toad. The driver tried his best, but the engine just wasn't fast enough. So, Toad **jumped** from the train and hid in the woods.

In the morning, Toad set off for home. As he walked by the canal, a woman on a barge called, **"Good morning!"** Toad, who was still dressed as a washerwoman, explained that he was lost. So, the woman offered him a lift, but she soon realised he was in disguise. She flung him into the water with a great big SPLASH!

Then, Toad saw the very car he had stolen and was sure he would be arrested. Instead, the drivers believed that he was a poor, ill washerwoman and put him in the car. **"I feel much better,"** said Toad. He added, **"Can I try driving?"** They laughed and nodded. Toad went faster and faster until he lost control and...

... CRASH!

He steered the car into the river.

The drivers and the police cried loudly behind Toad as the current carried him towards a dark hole in the riverbank. Then, he saw a pair of friendly eyes. **"Ratty!"** he spluttered.

"Come on," said Ratty, pulling Toad out. **"I've got something to tell you."**

Ratty explained that the weasels had taken over Toad Hall. But Badger had a secret plan. **"I knew your father, Toad,"** he explained. **"He discovered a tunnel that goes from the riverbank right up into Toad Hall!"** So, Ratty, Mole and Toad prepared their sticks and swords, then followed Badger through the darkness until they reached a trapdoor.

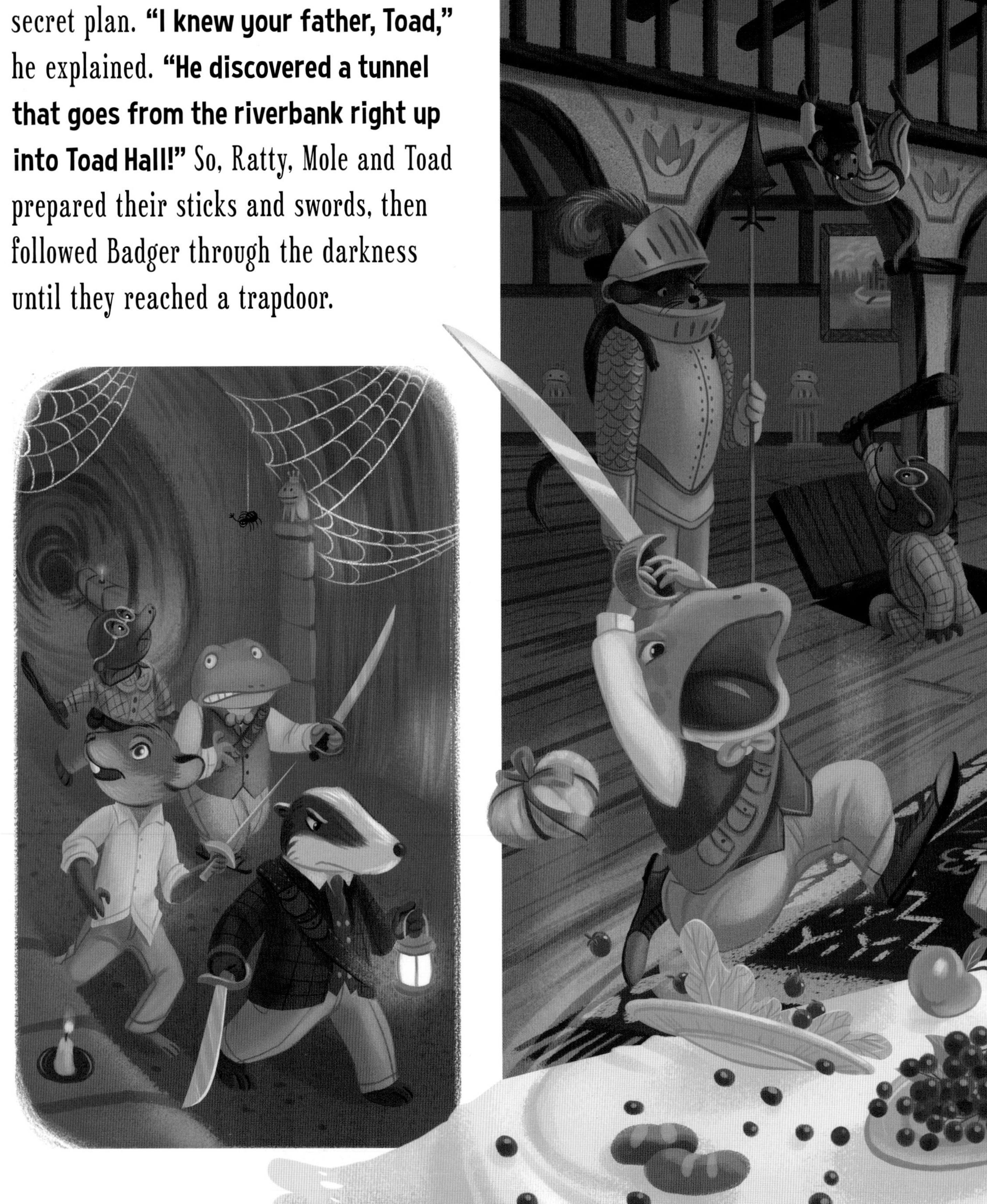

When the four friends peeked through the door, they saw their enemies celebrating the chief weasel's birthday in the Great Hall. Suddenly, Badger cried, **"Now!"** and the animals burst in, swishing their weapons around and yelling. The weasels were so frightened that they ran away, squeaking and squealing until none were left.

Toad held a big party to celebrate at Toad Hall. Ratty made him promise to change his ways, and to find and repay anyone that he had ever wronged. From that very day on, Toad, Ratty, Mole and Badger lived peacefully along the beautiful riverside together.